TOP 10 TWENTY-FIRST CENTURY ATHLETES

BY CRAIG ELLENPORT

Published by The Child's World®
1980 Lookout Drive • Mankato, MN 56003-1705
800-599-READ • www.childsworld.com

Photo credits:
Cover: Pixattitude/Dreamstime.com (3).
Interior: Dreamstime.com: Penchan Pumila 21 21. Newscom: Mingo Nesmith/Icon Sportswire 6; Jon SooHoo/UPI 7; Brian Rothmuller/Icon Sportswire 4, 10; John Angelillo/UPI 5, 13, 18; Jeff Siner/TNS 11; Christine Chew/UPI 14; Aaron Josefczyk/UPI 15; Steven Shaver/UPI 16; Kevin Dietsch/UPI 17; Hugh Philpott/UPI 19. Joe Robbins: 8, 9, 12.

ISBN: 9781503827240
LCCN: 2017960467

Printed in the United States of America
PA02380

CONTENTS

INTRODUCTION

WHO'S NUMBER ONE?

Bigger. Stronger. Faster. Many experts will tell you that today's pro athletes are in better shape than ever. Training is better. Athletes eat better food. The gear they use is the best yet.

So let's say that modern athletes are the best we've ever seen. Who is the No. 1 athlete of the 21st century? Starting in 2000, which person stands atop the sports world?

Coming up with that Top 10 list can be tricky. How can you compare athletes in a team sport with solo athletes? How do you compare a male football player with a female tennis star? What's more important, team championships or individual awards?

The 10 sports stars featured in this book are certainly among the best. Are they the ones you would choose?

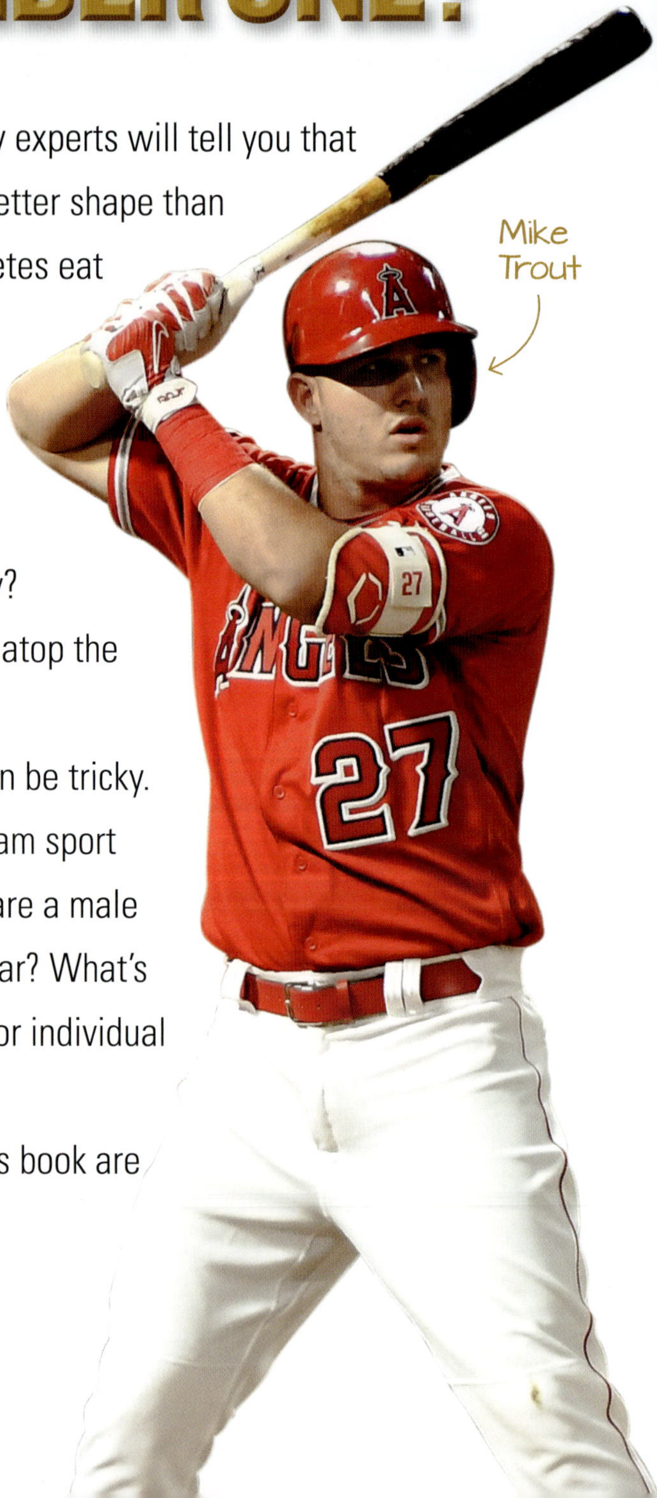

Mike Trout

That's what's fun about lists like this. There are no wrong answers! If you have an opinion and can back it up with facts, you can make your case. Talk to your friends. Did we leave anyone out? Who would you remove? And, most importantly, who's No. 1?

Read over the facts and stories about each athlete. You can also do research on your own. When you're done, decide your Top 10 list. The good thing about 21st century stars is that we get to keep watching them!

Serena Williams

NUMBERS, NUMBERS

What About the 1900s?

In 1999, ESPN named these people the top five athletes of the 20th century (1900-1999).

1. Michael Jordan (basketball)
2. Babe Ruth (baseball)
3. Muhammad Ali (boxing)
4. Jim Brown (football)
5. Wayne Gretzky (hockey)

SUE BIRD

BASKETBALL

From college to the pros to the Olympics, Sue Bird has always been a winner. She won a college championship, an WNBA title, and an Olympic gold medal!

She has won each of those amazing honors more than once. Bird led the University of Connecticut to the NCAA title in 2000 and 2002. In 2004 and 2010, she has helped the Storm win the WNBA crown. Playing for Team USA in the Olympics, Bird has helped bring home the gold *four* times!

As a **point guard**, Bird's job is passing the ball to teammates. In the WNBA, nobody is better at that than Bird. She has led the league in assists three times. In 2017, Bird became the league's all-time leader in assists, with 2,610!

Bird won an award as the best women's college point guard three times!

NUMBERS, NUMBERS

- Bird has been named to the WNBA All-Star Game 10 times.
- Bird ranks in the WNBA top 10 all-time in 3-pointers (fourth), steals (eighth), and total points (ninth).

KOBE BRYANT

BASKETBALL

When Bryant was six, he moved with his family to Italy. They lived there for seven years. Thanks to this, Bryant speaks fluent Italian!

Which NBA player would you want taking the final shot with the game on the line? For a decade, the answer was Kobe Bryant. He was a guard who could score from anywhere on the court. He was more than just clutch. He is one of the most successful players in NBA history.

Bryant played 20 seasons with the Los Angeles Lakers. He helped them win three NBA titles from 2000 to 2002. Bryant shared the spotlight on those teams with another superstar, Shaquille O'Neal. After O'Neal left the Lakers, Bryant led the team to two more NBA titles in 2009 and 2010. Bryant was named Finals MVP both times!

Bryant finished his career ranked third all-time in scoring.

NUMBERS, NUMBERS

- Bryant is the only player in NBA history to have two different jersey numbers retired by the same team. He wore No. 8 for the first 10 seasons. He switched to No. 24 in 2006.
- On January 22, 2006, Bryant scored 81 points against the Toronto Raptors. That's the second-best single-game point total in NBA history!

PEYTON MANNING

FOOTBALL

QB Peyton Manning was a smart player and great team leader. He turned the Indianapolis Colts into a top team. Along the way, he became the NFL's all-time leader in career passing yards and TD passes. Manning led the Colts to the playoffs in 11 of his 13 seasons. At the end of the 2006 season, he helped them win Super Bowl XLI. He was named Super Bowl MVP!

Manning missed 2011 with a neck injury. He signed with the Denver Broncos and won his fifth NFL MVP award in 2013. That's the most ever by one player. Two years later, in his final season, he helped the Broncos win Super Bowl 50!

Peyton's dad Archie played QB in the NFL for 14 seasons. Peyton's brother Eli is the longtime QB of the New York Giants.

NUMBERS, NUMBERS

Manning holds many spots on the all-time stats list:

Touchdowns: 539 (first)

Passing Yards: 71,940 (first)

Completions: 6,125 (third)

Attempts: 9,380 (second)

Plus, in 2013, Manning set the NFL single-season records for most passing yards (5,477) and most touchdown passes (55).

ALBERT PUJOLS

BASEBALL

Albert Pujols is one of the greatest home run hitters in baseball history. He is a slugger who can also hit for average. In 2001, he hit .329 with 37 homers and 130 runs batted in (RBI). He was named National League (NL) Rookie of the Year. Two years later, he led the NL with a .359 average.

As a first baseman, Pujols won two **Gold Glove** awards for excellent fielding. His hitting was even better. This great all-around star was named NL Most Valuable Player three times. He helped the St. Louis Cardinals win the World Series in 2006 and 2011.

Pujols signed with the Los Angeles Angels in 2012. He continued to blast homer after homer. In 2017, he hit his 600th homer. He finished the 2017 season with 614 home runs. That's seventh most in baseball history!

Pujols was born in the Dominican Republic. Many great baseball players are from there.

NUMBERS, NUMBERS

- Pujols had 100 or more RBI each of his first 10 seasons in the majors. Only Hall of Famer Al Simmons (11 seasons) had a longer streak.
- Pujols has 14 total seasons with 100 or more RBI. That's tied for the MLB record with Alex Rodriguez.

MIKE TROUT

BASEBALL

This Los Angeles Angels star was only eight years old when the 21st century began! Mike Trout didn't play his first full big-league season until 2012. Even though that's just a small part of the 2000s, Trout has done enough to make this Top 10.

A great player can hit for power and average. He can run the bases like a deer and field his position perfectly. Trout can do all that and more. As a 21-year-old rookie in 2012, Trout batted .326 with 30 home runs. He led the American League with 49 stolen bases and 129 runs. He was named AL Rookie of the Year and finished second in the AL MVP voting.

From 2012 to 2016, he finished in the top two of the MVP voting five years in a row! Most experts call him the best player in the game.

NUMBERS, NUMBERS

Mike Trout's MVP History

2017: Fourth*

2016: First

2015: Second

2014: First

2013: Second

2012: Second

*(*Trout missed 48 games and STILL finished fourth!)*

TIGER WOODS

GOLF

When the 21st century began, Tiger Woods was the top-ranked golfer in the world. He was only 24 years old. By 2017, he had become one of the greatest golfers in history!

Woods earned the No. 1 world ranking in August 1999. He held it until September 2004. Then he held the top spot from 2005 to 2010! No golfer has ever been ranked No. 1 as long as Woods. Along the way, he won 79 **PGA** tournaments. That is the second most all-time. Woods has done his best in golf's majors. Those are the four most important tournaments. Woods has won 14, second most ever.

Woods's real first name is Eldrick. His father gave him the nickname "Tiger." The name was in honor of a friend who fought with Tiger's dad in the Vietnam War.

NUMBERS, NUMBERS

Tiger's Major Wins

Tournament	Wins
Masters	4
US Open	3
British Open	3
PGA Championship	4

TOM BRADY

FOOTBALL

Early in the 2001 season, New England Patriots quarterback Drew Bledsoe was injured. Few people had high hopes for his backup, Tom Brady. Brady was in his second NFL season. He was a sixth-round **draft pick**—the 199th player taken in the 2000 draft. Brady took over for Bledsoe and did his best. Nobody could have imagined that Brady would become the most successful quarterback in NFL history!

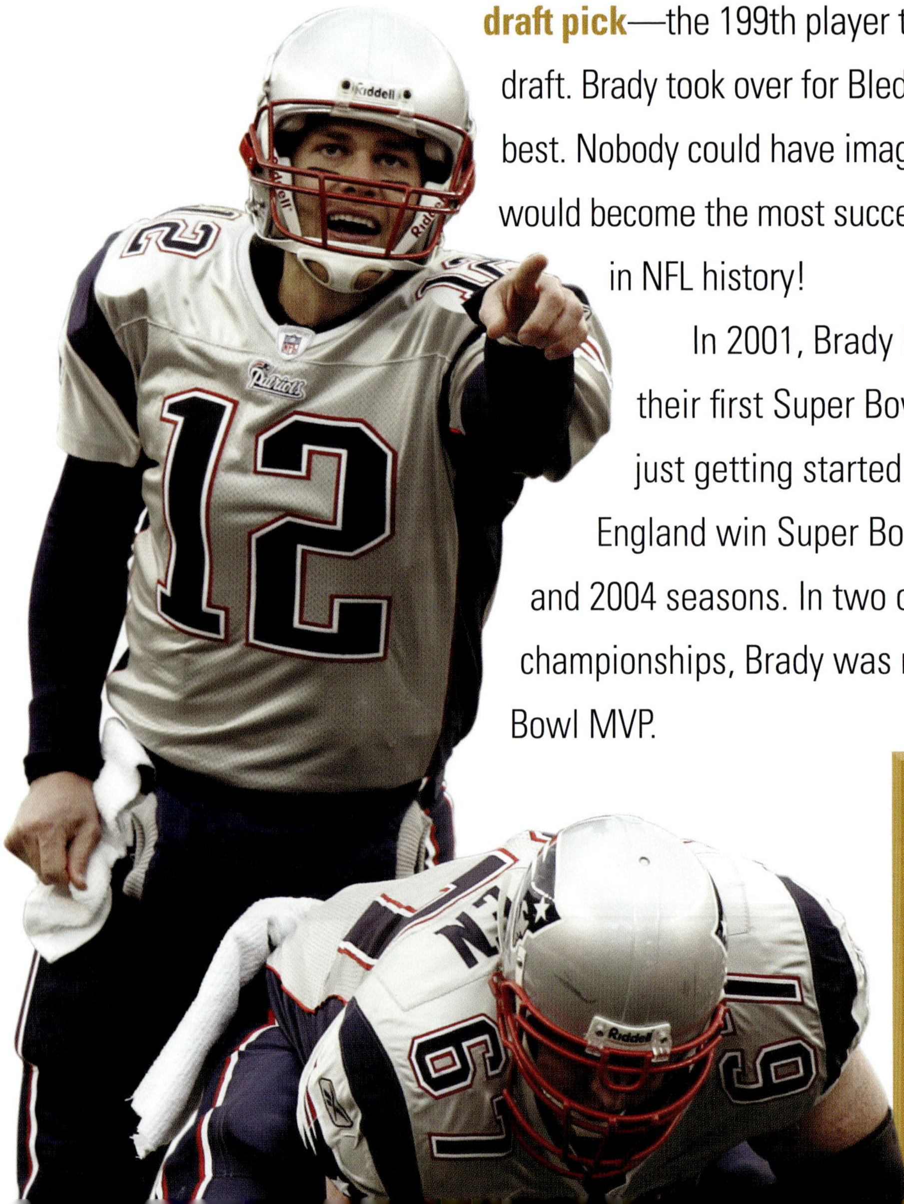

In 2001, Brady led the Patriots to their first Super Bowl title. He was just getting started. He helped New England win Super Bowls after the 2003 and 2004 seasons. In two of those three championships, Brady was named Super Bowl MVP.

NUMBERS, NUMBERS

Brady's All-Time Records	
Wins by a QB	196
Super Bowl TD passes	18
Super Bowl passing yards	505
Super Bowl MVP awards	4
Super Bowl wins	5

Hundreds of NFL quarterbacks have passed for 300 yards in a game. Tom Brady is the only one who has done it in three different countries (United States, Brita, Mexico).

Since Brady became the starter in 2001, the Patriots have never had a losing record. In 2007, Brady set many passing records, including throwing 50 touchdown passes. The Patriots became the first team in NFL history to finish the regular season with a 16-0 record. They lost the Super Bowl that season, but they continued to be one of the top teams in the league.

Brady works very hard to take care of himself all year long. He follows a very healthy diet and exercise plan. He has stayed in excellent condition at an age when most quarterbacks are retired. At 37, Brady led the Patriots to a win in Super Bowl XLIX. In that game, Brady led the Patriots to the greatest comeback in Super Bowl history. He was the first player ever to win the Super Bowl MVP four times!

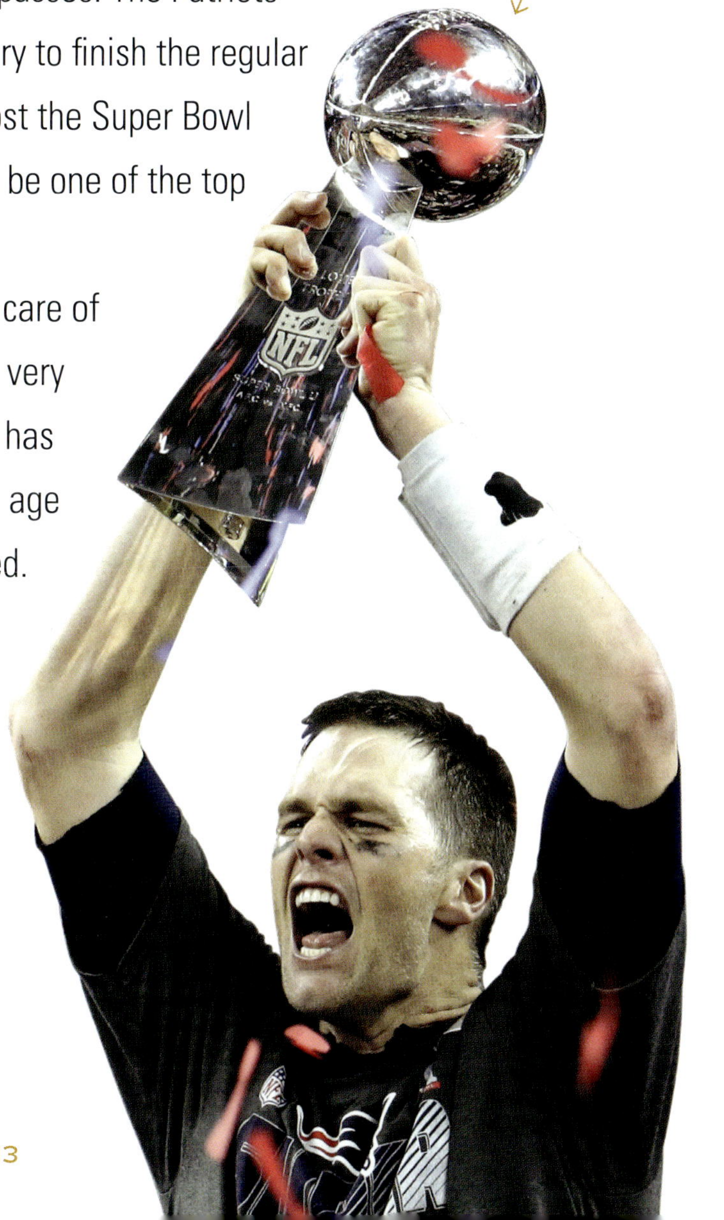

LEBRON JAMES

BASKETBALL

How good was young LeBron James? In high school, his team played in a college arena. That was to fit all the fans who wanted to see him. He was so good he jumped right from high school to the NBA. Once there, he became one of the greatest players in league history.

James was the first NBA draft pick in 2003. He was selected by his hometown team, the Cleveland Cavaliers. In 2007, he helped the Cavs reach the NBA Finals for the first time. A year later, James was named NBA MVP for the first time.

In addition to being a great scorer, James is one of the most **versatile** stars in the NBA. He has often led his team in points, rebounds, assists, and steals.

In 2010, James became a **free agent** and signed with the Miami Heat.

In 2002, James was named the high school National Player of the Year. He was the first junior to win. As a senior in 2003, he became the first player to win the award twice.

There he teamed with stars Dwyane Wade and Chris Bosh. That great trio led the Heat to the NBA Finals four years in a row. They won in 2012 and 2013.

In 2014, James made a joyful return to Cleveland. He took the Cavaliers to three straight NBA Finals. In 2016, they were down three games to one in the NBA Finals to Golden State. James took control. He scored 41 points in back-to-back wins. In Game 7, James had a triple-double (27 points, 11 rebounds, 11 assists). That gave Cleveland its first NBA title and James his third.

Overall, James has been NBA Finals MVP three times and NBA MVP four times. The only players who have won more MVPs are Hall of Famers Bill Russell, Kareem Abdul-Jabbar, and Michael Jordan.

NUMBERS, NUMBERS

- James holds the NBA career playoff scoring record with 6,136 points.
- James has made 80 3-pointers and 9 triple-doubles in the NBA Finals. Both are NBA career records.

MICHAEL PHELPS

SWIMMING

Michael Phelps grew up with **ADHD**. He couldn't focus in school and often got into trouble. When he was seven, his mom started him in swimming. She hoped the water would be calming for him. Phelps didn't like the pool at first. Soon, though, he began to love it. He found that he could really focus on swimming. After many years of hard work and success, he became the greatest swimmer of all time!

He was 15 years old at the 2000 Olympics in Sydney, Australia. He was the youngest athlete in 68 years to make the men's U.S. Olympic swim team. Phelps didn't win any medals in Sydney, but he made up for it in the years to come.

At the 2004 Olympics in Athens, Greece, Michael Phelps won six gold medals. Four years later in Beijing, China, Phelps won eight gold medals. Winning this many gold medals at one Olympic Games broke the record set by U.S. swimmer Mark Spitz in 1972. Believe it or not, Phelps wasn't done yet!

He competed in two more Olympics (2012 and 2016). He won race after race. He swam freestyle, butterfly, and relays. When he finally finished, he had a total of 23 gold medals. That is WAY more than any other athlete in Olympic history! He also set 39 world records, more than any other swimmer.

Phelps won eight gold medals in 2008. That year, he was named Sports Illustrated Sportsman of the Year. SI has named a Sportsman of the Year since 1954. Phelps is the only swimmer ever to win the honor!

NUMBERS, NUMBERS

Gold for Phelps!

Freestyle: 1

Butterfly: 6

Medley: 6

Relay Team: 10

SERENA WILLIAMS

TENNIS

Early in her career, Serena Williams wasn't even the top-ranked tennis player in her own family. Her older sister, Venus Williams, was ranked higher. That wasn't the case for long. Serena Williams was on her way to becoming the greatest women's player of all time. Some think she may be the greatest player ever—male or female!

The sisters were born a year apart. Venus turned pro in the late 1990s. Serena followed soon after. Serena won her first Grand Slam tournament, the U.S. Open, in 1999. (The four Grand Slam tennis tournaments are the Australian, French, and U.S. Opens, and Wimbledon.)

NUMBERS, NUMBERS

Grand Slams for Williams

Tournament	Wins
Australian Open	7
French Open	3
Wimbledon	7
US Open	6

In 2002, Serena met Venus in the final at Wimbledon. Serena defeated Venus to take over the No. 1 ranking in women's tennis. The previous No. 1? Venus!

For the next 15 years, Serena Williams dominated the world of tennis. She is a great athlete, quick and powerful. She has a super-fast serve. Her forehand whips the ball across the net.

Williams has won 23 Grand Slam singles tournaments, most all-time. She is the only player, male or female, to win three of the four Grand Slam events six times! From 2013 to 2016, Williams held the No. 1 ranking for 186 weeks. That tied Steffi Graf for longest streak ever.

Serena and Venus Williams are one of the best doubles teams in tennis history. They have won a record 14 Grand Slam doubles championships.

YOUR TOP TEN!

In this book, we listed our Top 10 athletes of the 2000s. We gave you some facts and information about each player. Now it's your turn to put the players in order. Find a pen and paper. Now make your own list! Who should be the No. 1 athlete of the 21st century (so far!)? How about your other nine choices? Would they be the same people? Would they be in the same order as they are in this book? Are any players missing from this book? Who would you include?

Remember, there are no wrong answers. Every fan might have different choices in a different order. Every fan should be able to back up their choices, though. If you need more information, go online and learn. Or find other books about these great players. Then discuss the choices with your friends!

THINK ABOUT THIS . . .

Here are some things to think about when making your own Top 10 list:

- How did each player accomplish his or her goals?
- How important were the championships or titles the player won?
- Did the player help change his or her sport?
- What were the player's different skills?

SPORTS GLOSSARY

ADHD short for a attention deficit and hyperactivity disorder, which causes people to have trouble focusing or getting work done

doubles (DUBB-els) in tennis, matches played by two teams of two players each

draft pick (DRAFT PIK) term given to players who are chosen by teams in the annual draft of new players for each sport

fluent (FLOO-ent) able to speak a language very well

free agent (FREE AY-jent) a player able to sign a contract with any team

Gold Glove (GOLD GLUV) an award given to the best fielders at each position in baseball

medley (MED-lee) a race in which swimmers use different strokes for each pair of laps

PGA short for Professional Golf Association, the group that puts on men's golf tournaments

point guard (POYNT GARD) a basketball position that brings the ball upcourt and passes to teammates, but also scores

QB short for quarterback, the key position in football

versatile (VERS-uh-tyl) able to do many things well

FIND OUT MORE

IN THE LIBRARY

Buckley Jr., James. *Who Are Venus and Serena Williams?* New York, NY: Penguin Workshop, 2017.

Nagelhout, Ryan. *Michael Phelps: Greatest Swimmer of All Time.* New York, NY: PowerKids Press, 2017.

Raum, Elizabeth. *LeBron James: Pro Sports Biographies.* Minneapolis, MN: Amicus Ink, 2016.

ON THE WEB

Visit our Web site for links about Top 10 21st-century athletes: **childsworld.com/links**

Note to Parents, Teachers, and Librarians: We routinely verify our Web links to make sure they are safe and active sites. So encourage your readers to check them out!

INDEX

ABOUT THE AUTHOR

Craig Ellenport is a veteran sports journalist who has been writing about sports for more than 20 years. He has written many books for young readers, and he helped the NFL launch its kids site, Playfootball.com. He lives in Massapequa, New York, with his wife and two sons, who aren't happy that he doesn't have any New York Mets players on this Top 10 list.